The

Book of

JACK

Written and Illustrated:

David Hall

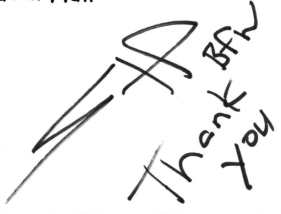

The BOOK of JACK

Table of Contents

I

POINDEXTER'S MILK MONEY

They caught me. My hands are shaking. Not from fear or the long chase. It's the sheer weight of running with a pack full of books. These two don't study or carry the load a real student like me does: my math book.

If I'd still had my backpack, maybe I could have gotten away. But Jack and Danny stole it from me last week. It's not like they needed my pack. The only thing they take home from school is a bad attitude. It was a cool red and blue Spider Man book bag with black spider webbing across the back. Well, as Mom would say, "Not a tear should fall over spilled milk," so I just told her that I lost it.

Dad's death over the summer hit me and mom pretty hard. This news--how come I have to run to school scared every day and that's why I'm so frightened of all these shadows--well, I'm just not going to tell her. She worries enough.

Due to Team Terror, Jack and Danny, school for many of us is hell. If you're little or just different, well then, you're eligible for special attention from Team Terror. Getting their attention is like winning a lottery no one wants to win.

It is Monday morning, and I'm Jack's first stop. His hands feel like vise grips and he's so much bigger than me. His thumbs and fingers are gouging into my flesh, blocking blood flow in my arms because he holds my upper arms so tightly.

Jack smiles sarcastically. "So how was your weekend Poindexter?"

I'm blushing and fidgeting, not because I'm embarrassed but because I hate this guy. Meanwhile, Danny is ruffling through my pockets, like in a cop show.

He is turning my pockets inside out. "OK, Poindexter, where is it!?"

If I acted like I had no idea what he was talking about, that would just tick him off. Earlier I'd had the bright idea to hide it in the only place they would never look. That's my math book. But my arms are turning purple, and the book is spine up in the dirt with my homework set free by the wind and sailing down the street.

By the way "it" is my milk money. Mom gives it to me like clockwork, every Monday morning before school. Well, as you can see, the cash never makes it to school.

Jack's smile never leaves. "I'm going to give you two choices. One is the easy choice, and many choose this one. That is, just give me your money. Or there's number two: hold out and we beat the hell out of you, and you still give me the money. Your choice, dude, what's it gonna be?" His hands tighten around my arms as he repeats, "Which will it be?"

Danny puts his hands around his mouth like a funnel. "Go for two! Come on, Poindexter. Go for two!"

The pain is too much. I grit my teeth and cry out, as I'm looking up at Jack, "It's in my math book!" Man, am I weak!

Danny bends over and pulls up my math book by the cover. He doesn't even bother to flip through it. He just shakes it and a crisp new $5 bill floats out and twirls to the ground. Then he throws my math book in the bushes as he picks up the five dollars. Then he holds it up on both edges and pops it.

"Good choice, Poindexter." Jack's hands loosen. He releases my tired arms. He stares at me for a few seconds then pushes me down. "Next week, let's dispense with the chase. You just bring it by the house, OK?"

I pause. He yells, "DID YOU HEAR ME, KID? Did you hear me, POINDEXTER?"

I think to myself, "Why do they keep calling me Poindexter?" I snap out of it. "Yeah, yeah, I hear ya."

They kick at some of the loose paper that once was my homework as they lumber away, monsters of the playground. I crawl around in the gravel and try to retrieve my work.

That's a typical Monday morning for me. That night my dreams brought me to a time when the world wasn't laughing at me. Jack and Danny didn't so much as look twice in my direction. The playground was no longer a war zone. Kids cried out for joy. Pain was no longer a factor. It was just a dream, but a good one.

The week quickly ended and not a second too soon.

II
THE ANSWER

Mom always takes me to this comic bookstore across town. She gives me enough money to buy my favorite comic book. Right in the same block is the beauty salon that she goes to every Saturday. This area is known as the dangerous side of town. The buildings are all old and dingy, and the sidewalks are narrow with cracks streaming everywhere. The old brick buildings look as though they are barely standing. The front windows of the closed shops are painted over. The paint is old with bare spots that reveal the darkness inside the vacant buildings.

The beauty shop block only has three stores open. The rest of the twenty places have been closed since long before I was born. First is my comic bookstore. Second is Mom's beauty salon. Third is an Indian bookstore.
Mom only lets me go buy comics. She told me to stay out of the Indian store. Well, an Indian bookstore didn't interest me anyway. I'd yet to walk over to see inside.

I was sitting on the curb in front of the beauty salon. The comic bookstore wasn't open yet. A shadow passes across the window of the Indian bookstore on the other side of the street. I see a man stand in front of the store. He is wearing a white turban, and his skin is dark brown. His khaki suit has no collar or tie. When he sees me out of the corner of his eye, he turns to face me in front of the plate glass window. The man smiles, then puts his hands together and bows his whole body. The only thing I can think of to do is wave back. He bows his head again, turns around and walks back into the shop. That alone is the strangest thing I've ever seen.

I sit on the curb and think about what Mom told me. But my curiosity is now too strong. Mom will never know if I don't tell her. So I get up and slowly walk across the street. The closer I get the more interesting the place looks. All the writing on the wall is in a different language. It looks like a hundred little drawings. Not one word can I understand, but I have to go in. It's like I have no choice. It's as if there's something in there I really need. I just don't know what it is yet.

My feet are making steps that my brain hasn't chosen. I'm a little nervous because the man's not the kind of person I've ever seen before. He looks nice enough, but I'm really surprised that I'm not scared. He looks at me as though he has something to say and by god I'm going to listen. He has the only screen door on the block. It's made of wood, and its hinges creak as I open it. A bell sounds ting-a-ling, ting-a-ling.

As I step in the door, a sweet smell overwhelms me. The man walks towards me slowly. "Oh, pleased to meet Young Sir." His large smile is contagious.

He bows again, with his hands joined as if in prayer. "Heaven has sent me joy, in such a small package."

The smell of cinnamon fills the room. It gently calms me. Books line the walls, interspersed with small glass jars. I am surrounded by huge dark barrels. The man's dark hands never separate, and his rigid body has a comfortable air to it.

"Oh, I see in the Young Sir's eyes one who runs from darkness."

I scratch my head. "You mean shadows?"

He lifts his hands up in the air, palms up. "My shadow proudly holds light up, as if to say "Old brother protects young brother." Light needs dark, oh, like baby needs mother. Young Sir's thoughts lead him away from the truth."

My eyes widen as my heart beats hard and my skin heats up. "The truth?" I ask.
His black eyes sparkle in the shop's dim light. "Your fear is not the darkness from which you run. It is what stands in it."
I still have no idea why I'm here, but I feel I will soon know. He puts his hands on my shoulders. "What is your wish, Young Sir? The one that holds your dreams..."
I think about it for a while and what comes to mind is Dad, I want Dad back, but I know he can't pull that off. So, I think harder. Then it finally came to me.

"Jack. Yeah, Jack. I just wish Jack would stop being so bad all the time."
He turns around and walks farther into the store. He walks behind the back counter and into a room. After a while, he comes out with a black wooden box in his hands. He sets it down on the counter. The box looks like it's a million years old. He blows the dust off the top and says, "Oh, Young Sir, souls are not always bad. In some lives they just need to be led in the right direction."
I put my hand on top of the box. "What is it?"

He looks down at me. "Oh, but it is your answer, Young Sir."

I look at the side. "My answer... How can this be my answer? It's just a box."

"Yes, Young Sir, it is just a box. But what is inside will fill your needs."

The scratched-up old wooden box had silver on the corners though they were tarnished and beat to heck. The corners made the black box look as if it were expensive in its day. It also had designs carved in it. The sides had hands inlaid in silver. The top had the symbol for mountains. If you held the box where the two hands were, on the south side was a symbol for water, two waves breaking towards the sides. And the north side of the box had a symbol for wind, four arrows breaking over a mountain, four lines streaking across a jet-black sky. Weird, they all just changed places.

The man kept brushing the old box all over with his bare hand. His fingernails were pink, almost white. They stood out because of his dark skin and the jet-black box.

I rested my arms on the glass counter. "What's in there? Is it dangerous? Will it hurt Jack?"

"I don't like the guy, but I definitely don't want to hurt him," I thought.

He smiled and put his hands over the box. "This is but a small thing that will do nothing more than just open his mind, Young Sir," he said.

Curiosity filled my mind even more. But I realized I had no way of paying for this. The contents of my pockets could only pay for a mere comic book.

"I have little money. How can I pay you?"

"The two dollars you have in your pocket is quite enough, Young Sir."

My hands fell to my side as I stepped back from the counter. "How did you know I have two dollars in my pocket?"

"The question is, Young Sir, how do I know your needs? How did I even know you would come today?"

A post stopped my backward motion with a thump. "Who are you? Are you a genie or something? Maybe you're a fortune teller?

Mom's going to be looking for me. Maybe I should go ..."

"Young Sir, the wish you desire lies in front of you. Going through that door now only prolongs the tyranny of his bad deeds. Young Sir knows that. Stay and relieve yourself of those bad deeds."

The guy has me there. I gather my bravery and step back up to the counter. He pushes the biggest star on the top of the box. The star sinks, and light shoots out from underneath his finger. The silver stars light up like Christmas tree lights, or as if they were different colored laser beams shooting into the sky. He waves his hand inches above the top, breaking the beams with his palm and fingers. The top of the box rises up and separates at the middle. White light shoots out in an ever-growing column. It lights the tops of his eye sockets and the bottom of his chin and nose in a ghostly way. His eyes never look up. They are hanging on the contents of the box, which is not yet visible. As the top of the box stops opening, his hands come to rest on the countertop. The edges of the lid drop towards the surface of the table. The light is still so bright that I can't even see the edges of the inside of the box.

The overwhelming light slowly dims as he reaches his hand inside. Finally it is extinguished, and he pulls out this dark brown leather book. The trim is almost black, and the paper is really a light brown, not white.

He reaches over to me with the book in his hands. I hesitate a little, but finally grab it.

"Young Sir, here is your answer."

"Just a book?" I look at him and the book, in disapproval.

He nods his head and closes his eyes slowly as he whips out a moon-shaped dagger with colorful gems on the handle. He holds the knife with one hand on the blade and the other underneath the handle. It's not often someone gives me a weapon to hold, so I drop the book and reach out to grab it quick like, thinking,

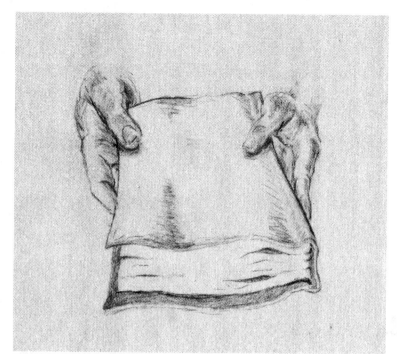

"*Yeah, this might stop Jack.*" I smile as I swing the sharp Indian dagger around in circles. Safety plays no part.

"What's this for?"

"A Moment, please ... Calm, Young Sir. Spirit."

I think that means settle down. So I did.

"Place the name of Young Sir in the darkness on the cover."

"With the knife?"

"The blade never forgets. It carves the memory into the book and then the book never forgets."

"Now?"

He nods slowly again. I hold the book down and dig the sharp edge into the cover, over and over. *P* is ugly, *O* is getting better, *I* almost legible, *N* and *D* are like cutting butter. As soon as I finish, he rips the knife out of my hand.

"When the book finds the hands of darkness, your reason for running will soon come to an end, Young Sir."

"I think the knife would work much better."

"Why use the blade when the pen is better suited? Young Sir." He puts his hand down on the scarred diary over my name, and the deep carving slowly disappears from underneath his majestic hand. It looks as though the print is writing itself in reverse as if an invisible eraser is peeling the name from the page. The cuts are pushing back together, as if they were never there. The hair on my neck is standing up and tickling my skin. My eyes are dry because I dare not blink for fear of missing something.

"How did you do that? Are you magic? Can you do anything you want?" I exclaim.

As he lifts his hands from the book, a dark print remains as if it is burned on. He puts his hand on my chest, and I begin to shake uncontrollably. Suddenly, the handprint on the cover gradually dissolves as if it is a light coating of water slowly evaporating into the air. I can't move away, because my muscles are lightly twitching underneath the man's palm. His smile calms me and eliminates my fear. Slowly he pulls his large palm from my chest. I stumble back, as if I have tumbled over something that doesn't exist.

"Young Sir, the book needs only to be put into the boy's hands, and the rest will find its own way."

"So I give it to him?"

"It does not matter how he receives the gift, only that his hands touch the cover."

I put the book under my arm and dig into my pocket. The two dollars are gone. I check all pockets frantically as the man's smile deepens.

"Young Sir, payment has already been received." He opens his closed fist, palm up. Damned if my two dollars aren't already there. Man, he is so mysterious!

"Young Sir's Mom is waiting."

I want to ask how he knows that, but he hasn't answered any of my questions so far, so I don't think he's going to start now. He walks around the counter and puts his hands on my shoulder and pushes me towards the door.

"Young Sir, have a wonderful day. May all who teach you, teach you well."

The screen door shuts behind me. He stands inside with his hands behind his back. He gives me one last modest bow, then backs into the darkness of his shop.

My chest itches as I walk across the street. I pull the collar of my T-shirt down, and the massive handprint is still there, a pink reminder of today's strange events. I step up onto the curb as the overweight comic bookstore owner is lazily opening his door for the first time that day. Mom is coming out of the beauty shop with her new hairdo.

"Did you get your book, honey?"

I pat the cover and say, "Yes, ma'am."

On the way home, Mom was throwing her new hairdo around. Coke-can curls are slowly bouncing up and down as she laughs and talks about her new job.

"Now that I'm making more money, we can start doing more things together. And the two-dollar allowance, well, we can double that."

I think to myself, *"Now I can buy two of nothing instead of just one."* But I know she is trying as

20

hard as she can, so I give her the thumbs-up with the big smile.

"Oh, something I forgot." She reaches into the backseat of the car and ruffles around for a few minutes with her eyes on the road as we drive down the street.

"It's here somewhere."

"What is it, Mom?"

"Give me a minute," she says

The car weaves back and forth, and let me tell you, on the cross-town road, going fifty miles an hour, it's a little scary. She is throwing stuff around in the back seat, curlers and her makeup kit, dresses, and panty hose. It's a real closet back there. When she finally finds it, it's a crumpled paper bag that has something stiff and flat in it. She tosses it in my lap. I look down at the bag. "What is it?"

"You've got eyes, use 'em."

I open the brown paper bag, and inside is a jet-black backpack.

Cool, I'm really getting tired of carrying my 300-pound math book to school. Let's not even talk about my 600-pound history book.

Mom suddenly pulls her car to the side of the road. She takes her well-groomed thumb and puts it underneath my eye, then gently forces it open and looks into them. Her finger nails are bright red and three miles long.

"Oh my god, when was the last time?" She pauses and looks at me seriously.

I'm thinking maybe she found out, maybe she knows that I went over to the Indian store. Maybe he did something to me. Maybe I'm sick! Oh God, what's wrong? Am I dying?

"I'm sorry, Mom. I promise I'll ..."

She cuts me off as she looks at me very seriously.

"You won't do what, honey?" She keeps glaring into my eyes, investigating, moving her head back and forth. Her serious face goes blank. And then a smile creeps up onto it.

"When was the last time you had some ice cream? I'm afraid if we don't get some ice cream in you, in the next few minutes, you might not survive. I don't think I could live with myself if that happens."

Relief comes over me. I thought she'd figured it out. My panicked guilty face was not ready to smile, nor was my guilty heart relieved. I wasn't about to tell Mom where I'd been, because I knew it wouldn't be the last time I'd see him.

III
"I'M NOT A BAD GUY"

I'm Jack. I'm not a bad guy. If you're not stepping on someone they will just turn around and jump up and down on your head. So, I just jump first, that's all ...

I have a Spider Man backpack underneath my bed with a bundle of cash inside it. It has years of my collections, collections of milk money, that is. I'm weeks away from the prize. The prize is a slightly used air rifle with a mile-long scope and a carved oak handle. The guy selling it, his name is Delbert. He's a real ugly hillbilly-lookin' guy who works for Dad. His long dirty hair bunches up in his oily face. Each time a wad of unkempt hair runs across his thick glasses, it leaves a grease trail. As I talk to him, he's always pulling his glasses off and cleaning them on the dirty T-shirt he's wearing. I thought about telling the smelly guy, if you just take a bath you wouldn't need to clean your glasses so much. But if I piss him off, I won't get the gun. You ask why does Jack need a gun? Well, Jack needs people to listen to him! That's why Jack needs a gun. The neighbors always stare at me then chase me away. In my neighborhood and all around the town, I have to watch my step, because no one likes me. My only friend hangs out with me because if he didn't I would find him, then kick his butt. I have money and power and that's just fine. That's all a guy needs. Who needs true friends, when one can be bought?

Monday morning I start my rounds. My first stop is this little kid, I don't even know his name, and I really don't care. Every Monday morning he comes up with his $5 protection fee. About three weeks ago I took the poor bastard's backpack. I know that was hard for him to part with because the little Poindexter always carries his weight in schoolbooks. Geeks like him are my meat and gravy. Even when they put up a fight, a stiff wind can beat them.

Poindexter's just one of my many daily conquests. Today I'm trying something new. Normally I go find him, but I'm bored with that. I ordered him to bring my prize to me, and under stress he submitted. I walk out onto the porch and wait for my spoils, when Danny walks up. I'm sitting at the end of the porch on the swinging bench that hangs from the ceiling by four little chains. The two hooks at the top squeak as I swing back and forth sitting in the middle of the wooden bench, the throne in the Kingdom of Jack.

Danny slowly walks up the steps. The bare wood creaks as he reaches my presence. The king's loyal servant enters my throne room. Short of bowing and taking a knee, my loyal follower shows his obedience in his face and actions.

He puts his head down slowly and says "Hey, man." And I answer "Hey, man." Then he sits down on the brick railing around my porch and looks through a window into the living room.

"Are you ready to go yet?"

I look at the side of his head because he dares not look at me.

"I'm waiting for Spider-pack boy."

"Spider-pack boy? What do you mean, Spider-pack boy?"

"You remember, the kid with the backpack."

"Oh yeah, Poindexter." Danny looks at me and smiles. "What makes you think he's coming?"

"Because I told him!" I glare at Danny's sheeplike eyes.

We sat there for twenty minutes till it became obvious: Poindexter wasn't coming. Danny impatiently says, "He ain't coming."

I agree. "Maybe we can cut him off at the park."

So we run. I sure didn't want to get out of breath today. Each time the bottoms of my tennis shoes hit the ground, it multiplies my anger. When we arrive at the park, sweat is dripping off my forehead.

The trees are fairly dense in the park. We hide behind one and wait for Poindexter to come down the path.

From a distance I see someone. I can't tell if it's him. Then Danny, looking at him from the other side of the tree, says, "It's him, it's him!"

I push Danny out from behind the tree and tell him to run around the backside of the woods and cut him off. He does it while I wait. The boy meanders along slowly. I step out from behind the tree as he gets close enough. When Poindexter sees me, he jumps back. He quickly turns around, but to his surprise, Danny appears out of the blue, right in front of him. Danny grabs him by the collar and pushes him with his closed fist towards me.

Danny stares down at the boy, "Did you forget something this morning?" Danny's body eclipses Poindexter, who is like a baby taking his first step looking up the front grill of a semi trailer truck.

Poindexter crumples a bit. "I don't think so," he says.

Danny still has a fistful of the boy's collar. He pushes him again, "Are you sure?"

"Quit playing with him, Danny!" I didn't feel like giving him the same two options I let him have last time.

As I walk closer to Poindexter, Danny releases his collar. When I get close enough, I plant one in his face. The boy falls backwards, then stumbles and lands face down in the dirt.

Looking down at Poindexter, I say, "I told you to bring it by the house, but no, you didn't listen. And here we are going with option two."

The kid rises up on his elbow, dirt-filled tears rolling off his cheeks. He cries out, then shifts his weight again as he begins to drive his hands deep into his pockets.

"I'm sorry, Jack. I'll never do it again!"

Poindexter's arms quiver. Obviously, he can't find the money. He pulls the black over-filled backpack off his shoulders. His hands are running through its contents. Danny loses patience. He bends over and grabs the backpack out of his hands.

Poindexter fights back. "No!"

Danny pulls the backpack away and the kid plays a losing game of tug-o-war.

Danny's free hand grabs the kid's arm. "If you don't let go, I'm gonna sock you again!"

Poindexter crumples on the ground, defeated again. Danny slings the backpack over to me. I unzip it and begin to dump everything out.

I turn to the whimpering kid and say. "Why are you carrying this useless crap?"

The kid's papers float down. At the same time his books plop out onto the ground one at a time. He lies there and cries but doesn't answer. Soon the pack is empty, but the money isn't there.

I yell at him. "Where is the money? You little geek!" Tears not yet dry, the boy smiles and says, "It's in the diary."

So I bend over and launch his math book into the trees. Underneath is a brown diary. I quickly snatch it off the ground. It's open face down. Five $1 bills are shoved between the pages.

I pull them out and stuff them into my pocket, then close the book. It's a really cool looking leather book that seems to be very old. My hands begin to tremble, and then my arms.

Danny looks at me. "Are you OK, man?"

The leather around my thumbs darkens and balloons out as if the cover is burning. I want to let the book go, but it's as if the diary is holding me.

Danny again yells, "Are you OK?"

He walks up and puts his hand on my shoulder, then draws it back as if he'd had a shock. He falls back onto the ground and crawls away from me. His scared expression is the last I see of him before he jumps up and runs away.

Soon the book cover is completely dark brown, almost black. I can't do anything but look down at it. The brown fades back to its normal shade, but before I could let the book go, it appears as though something is being carved on the front of it. An invisible knife is slowly being dragged across the cover. First I see an ugly half loop. Two strokes follow. All of a sudden a line runs through them. It's a J, next an A, then a C--it's JACK! I look up at the kid lying on the ground. His smile is understandable now. How did he do this to me? What is going on here?

IV
GETTING TO KNOW THE BOOK

It's not stopping. I still can't let go of that book. Suddenly I am crumpling down to my knees and the book falls to the ground. As Poindexter gathers his things, I have the urge to pluck him up and ask him what he did to me, but my muscles feel like ice and keep me from moving.

The last I see of him is the white soles of his shoes running off towards school. I sit there with my legs underneath me and the book lying in the grass with an ugly carving of my name on the cover. I wasn't about to pick it up.

My muscles slowly thaw, and I timidly crawl away from the book till I can get up and run. Looking back, I see the cover lying in the bright sunlight on the green grass.

Second hour has come. I've all but forgotten the morning's events when Danny walks up to me in the hall after the bell rings (he and I hardly ever make it to class on time). Standing in the hall, Danny calmly asks again, "Are you OK, man?"

I punch him in the chest, "What the heck happened to you? Thought you had my back, man!"

Danny cowers, "Man, I was just going to get help."

I yell, "I missed the class called 'I Am a Coward 101.' Where did you learn that?"

He backs up. "I didn't know what to do, so I just ran."

I walk away, not knowing if I'm angry at him or angry at myself for calling him a friend. The rest of the day flies by. I'm doing my rounds without Danny.

The last stop is old Lady Hillbloom's place. Behind her house in her long yard she has many fruit trees. I climb the rock wall behind the trees. The house is the oldest in my neighborhood, a four-story gray stone palace from a time long ago.

The huge structure has walls made of all different size rocks, and it has large windows shaped like bullets. It's been so long since the frames of the windows have been painted that the white paint is chipping off and the weathered wood shows through. Underneath the frames, running down the rocks, red stains ooze out as if the old house is crying blood from each window. I asked Dad about that and he told me it was rust from all the nails holding the old windows in. Hillbloom's husband was a famous military man. He built this house when the town was lots smaller and my neighborhood was a vacant hill. Now over a hundred houses have been built down below Hillbloom Manor.

Colonel Hillbloom constructed a fortress. Sneaking in to steal apples isn't easy. Most kids wouldn't dare sneak up to the old lady's house. Rumors about her being a witch or just plain evil didn't scare me. So every chance I have, I sneak up and take her apples. Truth be told, I've never actually seen her face.

It's a bright day. I peel off my shirt and begin to collect apples from the low-hanging branches. I stand on my tippy toes and jump around like a puppy jumping up in the air for a Frisbee. Then I hear from behind "You bad children! Stay off my property!" The voice is less than a step away, but I'm too scared to turn. I bend over and pick up my shirt, with the apples inside. "Those aren't yours!" she exclaims. I begin to run. I throw my shirt over the wall. I hear it go "thump thump thump thump thump." The old lady's voice is farther away, but louder: "You stay off my property or I'll sic the dogs on you!"

I know that's an empty threat because that's one thing I have seen, her ugly little dogs. And these beasts are no more than ankle biters. I bound the six-foot wall. It has many rocks to climb over. I get to the top and catch my shoe and tumble to the other side. "Thump!" I land on three rotten apples, turning them into apple sauce.

"Don't you ever come back!" Her voice comes from the far side of the wall. I laugh and tell her, "I'll come back any time I want, you old witch!" She quietly says, "If you do, I'll poison these apples and you'll die in your sleep." That was scary.

I yell, "You want these apples back, here you go." So I back up from the wall and start launching them back over.

She yells, "Stop--," but I pick up one of the apples and throw it as hard as I can. It goes up and up and through a third floor window, taking the rusty frame with it. The deep sound of breaking glass pours out into the backyard. "No--" the old lady cries out. "My husband built this house with his bare hands and now you're destroying it, you terrible child!" The sound of broken glass makes me run.

Dinner's at 5:00 and Dad accepts no excuses. So I head for home.

Dad's real strict but he never makes me do homework. He feels that we're a family of workers. He says I'm not going to college anyway. When I finish high school, I'll just be another construction worker or plumber, so Pop always says, "Who needs algebra or history?" The only thing I'm going to think about is paying rent and the bills when I get older.

My old wooden house has drafts through invisible holes. At night up on Hillbloom Drive the wind whistles through our house. Dad lights a flame in the undersized fireplace every night before bed. I lie in my room and dream about getting my new air rifle and shooting old lady Hillbloom's windows out.

The next day comes early as sounds of Dad throwing tools in the back of his truck wakes me up. I roll over on my side and my pillow seems to be extra lumpy. I reach under it and feel something.

I pull it out. It's the diary! I sling it across the room, hoping it doesn't grab me again. The old thing hits the wall and comes to rest on the ground.

"How did it get here?" I ask myself.

I snatch up my hockey stick and walk over to it. It looks safe enough, and I could never have imagined being afraid to pick up a book until now.

The soft leather cover lies motionless in the corner. I poke it with the stick. It doesn't so much as move, so I flip it over with the ugly end of my hockey stick. Inside the cover is a story about Poindexter! Black letters begin to fill the lines. It says, "My name is Jack. I'm from a small city called Fairmont." I kneel down beside it and begin to rub my head. What's going on here? The damn thing is writing stuff about me!

The ugly chicken scratch is big and running over each line, but it's oddly understandable. Wait a sec. It's my handwriting!

It starts writing again. "The things I've done I'm not proud of, but I do them because I don't know any better. Yesterday morning I beat a kid up and took his milk money. I knew it wasn't right, but I did it anyway. After that I pushed another kid down in the lunchroom and took his dessert and his pride. After school I went to the convenience store to steal a candy bar and a pack of gum.

"For most kids that would've been a full day, but not for me. I went up to old lady Hillbloom's house and stole her apples and broke out her window. But I did not dare to be late for dinner, so I ran home. If Dad ever finds out what I've done, I will surely never see the light of day again. But I promise myself, if I don't change, I will tell Dad myself!"

Now that's NOT something I would say. No way I'd say something like that. What's going on here? I close the book up and run with it to the living room, I pass Mom without even saying "Good morning." The fireplace is crackling with fresh flames. I take the evidence and toss it in the flames. I'm watching each page burn till they turn black and drift upwards. The orange and yellow flames swallow each page. Then the fire crackles louder as the cover also begins to burn. Soon it's gone too.

I took care of the problem. Leaving that kind of evidence around could only lead to my quick downfall. Dad would jump all over me for lesser crimes. So, my activities have to be kept on the hush hush.

Mom makes me oatmeal. "What are your plans today, Jack?"

I look at her seriously. "Well, Mom, I think I might create mayhem today." Then I smile. "Maybe burn the school down, pull a girl's hair or two, and beat some kid up just for being smaller than me. How about you, Mom, what will you do today?"

She smiles, obviously not taking me seriously at all. "Well, I thought maybe I would start with the kitchen. Then the living room."

I blink my eyes and swallow in surprise. "You're going to burn the house down?" Mom rolls her eyes. "No, silly, I'm going to clean." She pauses and pushes my hair back. "You have the strangest little mind."

I think burning this pile of sticks down sounds more interesting than cleaning it. Well, that's why they pay her the big bucks. Danny stands out on the porch, but I'm still pissed at him. So I take the back door.

Thinking as I walk to school, I sure don't want to be thought of as a liar. So I set out to do what Mom and I talked about.

Let's see, what's first? Oh yeah, pull at least two girls hair. And as I'm walking in the front doors of school, I see them: There are two girls facing each other. These two supermodel wannabe's would rather jump from a moving car than talk to me. So I run up between them as they're talking about something real stupid. I reach behind them and pull both their hair at the same time. It looks as though they're both saying yes to me or maybe just looking up simultaneously. The screams and empty punches come way too late. I'm in the door before they can even realize what has happened to them. Hopefully, they're thinking, "Maybe we should've been nicer to him," or not. I notice they're chasing me. With my reputation, everyone knows I don't have to run. But I do anyway for fun. These two chase me halfway down the hall with their papers flying behind them. Their faces are angry and red as they hug their pre-college textbooks with both hands.

I come around the corner and stop. Then I kick open the boys' bathroom door. This poor unsuspecting tiny freak of nature is coming out at the same time. I hear his glasses or maybe his nose shattering with the weight of that swinging door. I yell out, "Here's Johnny!" Elf boy falls backwards onto the ground, without even a chance to be surprised.

The mad Barbies are rounding the corner. So I duck into the head. One of the Barbies yells, "My boyfriend is going to get you, Jack!" I know their boyfriends and I know I don't have anything to worry about. The kid on the floor is more dangerous than the two of them.

The mad Barbies push on the door. The boy is lying face up in front of me. "Hey, man, let me go. I didn't do anything to you!" he quietly mumbles. The door starts to open, then loudly shuts with the mass of my shoulder against it. The heavy wooden thing is slamming again and again as the mad Barbies try to get to me.

Obviously not concerned, I yell out in a jovial voice, "Tell him to bring it on, Barbie girl!"

The door stops jerking. "My new boyfriend is the quarterback of the high-school football team. You know, Iron Skull? I'll bet you didn't know that, did ya, Jack?" I'm not saying anything back, because if that's true, my ass is grass.

This guy is known for being the toughest quarterback ever in Fartville. One time he ran to the line of scrimmage and went head to head with an All State noseguard. Iron

Skull knocked his butt smooth out. They were picking the 300-pound lineman's teeth up off the ground.

I look down at the boy withering on the bathroom floor. I whisper, "Is that true?" He's halfway unconscious, but he shrugs his shoulders and says in a normal voice, "I don't know, man."

I place my pointer finger over my mouth. "Shhh..."

I look at him harder. The freak's glasses are hanging off both ears. The black frame is split right through the middle. He shuts right up for me.

Soon after, the first bell rings and we have five minutes till class. My little elf buddy gathers his things. I peek out to see if the coast is clear. It is. He gets up and walks to the door as he puts his broken glasses in a pocket.

I poke him in the chest. It pushes him back in and away from the door at the same time. I pull out some matches and slowly strike one. Then I calmly throw it in the trash. The boy begins to run at the door. I punch him in the breadbasket. He doubles over. Flames are rolling out of the trashcan. He's crying and asking me why. I bend over and jokingly whimper, "If you tell anyone what happened"--I wave my fist in front of his face--"Here's four more where that one came from."

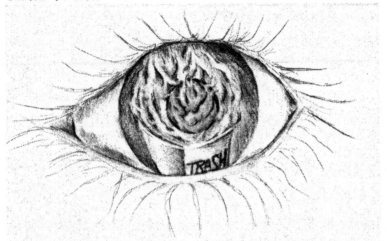

Man, am I good. All three projects completed before first hour, boy, babes and billowing flames. I walk out of the bathroom with flames and smoke billowing out behind me, and elf boy crawling to his first hour.

The uneventful day flows by. You just can't top the three-in-five-minutes thing.

At dinner, Dad says in between chews, "I need you to work this weekend."

"Oh, Dad, please don't make me go..."
Dad leans his head to the side and looks at me over the top of his glasses.
"You know we all pull our own weight around here!"
"But Dad..."
The old man glares at me as if to say, "Conversation over!"

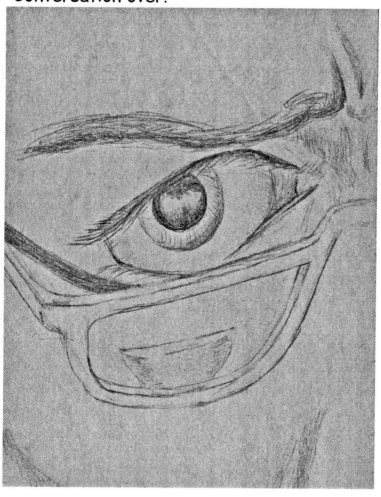

V

QUIETLY TALKING ABOUT DAD

Dad works so hard. The last day he had off was their wedding day. The guy lives for work and he can't understand when someone doesn't want to.

Dad's football trophies line the wall of this rickety old house. He had a minor injury that pushed him out of college ball. His work fills the empty spot. Dad's large body screams out "Athlete from Years Past." His oversize calloused fingers look like forked sticks. His yellow torn and jagged fingernails have the strength of ten. The old man's veins pop out so far I can see them pumping.

Mom pats my head. "It will be OK. I'll make your favorite lunch. Sound good?"

No! Not working sounds good to me, but that's the one thing about Dad, he won't take no for an answer. My mashed potatoes don't taste good anymore.

The work that Dad has for me, well, it sucks! He has a side job to build an extra room for some big-money guy on the rich side of town. Dad hired about fifty guys, and I'll be cleaning up after them, sweeping, picking up mysterious pieces of wood. I'll just be an all-around slave, and oh yeah, I don't get paid! Real fun.

I'm lying in bed thinking about all the work, when my eyes start closing. Since I'm not quite ready for sleep, I force them back open. Then I just give up and roll over on my side. My hand slides under the pillow. It's rudely stopped. My eyes fly open and suddenly I'm sitting up. I quickly look back down to the pillow. Afraid to move the soft haven, I just stare at it.

It's just a dang pillow, so I rip the mysteriously heavy thing from underneath. It is the diary! It looks as if I never... The dang thing is untouched! I'm so surprised at its healthy appearance that I flip through it. Not even a burned page! The handwriting is still there. Whoa! The diary begins to shake and twitch. I quickly drop it with the cover face up. It begins jumping up and down, leaping straight into the air. When the diary finally settles down, the cover flips open. The black writing is now glowing like it's gold.

The page bows slightly as if someone is turning it to the next one. Then the yellowed pages flatten out from the middle as if someone is smoothing the two open pages, preparing to write. Suddenly, the cursed diary begins to write again.

Scratch, scratch, scratch. Despite my own warning, I did it again. The diary lists it all, everything, leaving nothing out. As it writes, I get a cold feeling. The diary tells things I never knew. For example, the boy on the floor just had his appendix pulled out, and when I hit him, he had to go back to the hospital. The janitor got burned real bad putting out my fire.

But nothing about the Barbies. Somehow that's not a surprise.

I really never thought about the people I messed with or their feelings. To tell ya the truth, I never cared.

The last words written: "I'm going to stop doing these things. I'm going to be a better person because if I don't I will tell Dad." I say out loud. "Just how are you going to make do that?"

"Well, it's good that you ask." I drop the diary and crawl to the edge of my bed. It's talking to me!

I can hear the pen scratching words on the aged page. It is as if the sound is a voice telling me what it's writing. I have to look! So I move closer to the pulsating page moving up and down from the weight of an invisible hand.

Dad will wake up one day and there this book will be, next to his bed for him to read--my black and white truth.

I roll off my bed and grab my new diary and head for the flames again. The slightly green wood pops with yellow streams of anger. The book *can't* come back this time.

I tear off the first three pages and throw them on the fire. They're quickly swallowed up. Then I dump the book. It takes longer, but soon the diary is gone too.

I go back to my comfortable mattress, eager to join mom and dad sleeping. Still I hesitate even to touch my soft happy place. My pillow has a different feeling, as if each time I close my eyes, the damn thing socks me in the chops, real hard like. When you spend your whole life trying to convince yourself nothing can hurt you, you believe fear is something you give, not take. Well, this comfortable haven is now a fanged predator, preying on me. I'm just not ready to be the victim yet. So I grab the pillow off the sheets. Nothing, thank god! My head hits the dragon and sleep comes quick.

Soon morning light hits my face and makes the inside of my eyelids red. How the heck is it doing that? Well, sleep ends. I roll over, and it feels like my head is rolling up hill. Only one thing can do that. There's something under my pillow. I reach under, and it's the book! It can't be! I slowly inch the soft-covered book out. I can't kill this thing! My pillow drops off the bed as I shift my weight. The diary opens. Scratch, scratch, scratch, the damn thing is writing again! I slam it shut.

Slowly I slide it under my evil pillow. The pillow appears to be alive. The dang thing is rising up and falling down, over and over, like uncontrollable spasms. It's kinda freaky.

When Mom comes in, she will spot my energetic pillow right away. So I rip the magical lie detector out from under my pillow. The book jerks around in my hand trying to jump free. I drop to my knees and jam it under my mattress, thinking that would quiet the dang thing down. I plop on my tummy. As I lie on it, nothing happens. I roll over and lie flat on my back. I look up at the dirty walls. They're caked in dust. Mom says my room is so messy that not even she wants to work here. So she leaves me in peace most of the time. But Mom does make my bed. Thump, thump! It feels like someone is kicking the bottom of my mattress. Thump, thump… "Stop it!" I yell at the top of my lungs. But it doesn't slow down. I scream "Stop!" but the bed feels as if it is plugged into the wall, jumping around like I put a quarter in, ya know, like in the movies. I pull the diary out. It leaps free from my hand onto the mattress, open. Scratch, scratch, scratch.

The book says. "Jack…"

Mom steps into the doorway of my room. I slam the diary shut. Her cheek rises and her brow wrinkles. "Are you OK, honey?"

"Yes, Mom, I'm fine!" It's jerking around in my hands uncontrollably like a large animal in a small cage.

"Are you sure, sweetie?"

"Yes Mom, I'm fine. OK?"

She stares at me, and the book that's whipping around in my arms. "O-K, come to breakfast then." Mom walks out and shuts the door. A loud and bloody murder can take place in this house and she would never be the wiser.

The diary flies out of my hands again and slaps onto the sheets. Then the book jumps up and flaps open like a bird. It slowly falls back to my mattress and says. "Jack, you don't seem to understand, I'm not going to shut up until you straighten up!"

I think to myself, "Straighten up? I'm just fine. As a matter of fact, I'm perfect. Yeah, perfection."

Scratch, scratch, scratch. "Shut up, Jack! You're a perfect mess. Not one person likes you. The only reason people talk to you is they're scared, or they're related. Jack, wake up!"

I poke the page real hard and yell, "No one talks like that to me!"

In bold oversized letters the diary answers. "I'M GIVING YOU ONE MORE CHANCE..."

I sit there stewing for quite a while. It starts again, "I'm only giving you one more chance, Jack. If you blow this one, that's it."

Slamming my hand down on the soft pages, I protest, "You can't tell me what to do!"

The page flips. "Well, maybe not, but Dad will have something interesting to read if you don't."

"Why are you doing this?"

"Because there's a new sheriff in town and you can't lie to this one."

That was no answer. I close the book. It doesn't move.

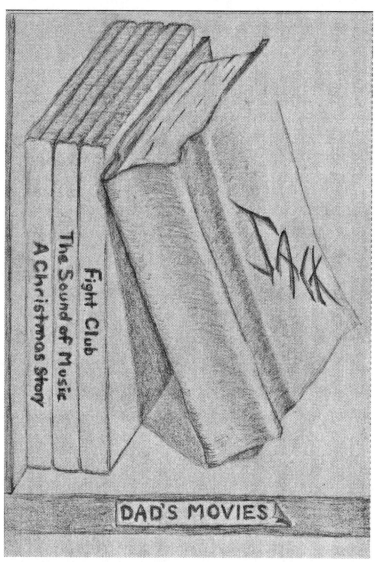

I can't let Dad find out, so I whip out my Spider Man backpack and unload the cash into a shoebox. I put my captor inside and sling the pack on my back. The idea is to give the book bag to Poindexter. Mom has her normal breakfast spread out. I run through the living room.

"I've got to go, Mom. See you later!"

As I'm turning the door handle, she runs into the room. "No, you don't, get your butt back in here!"

The angry housewife points at the door. "Close it."

"But Mom..."

She stomps her foot. "Now!"

I curl my lip and murmur, "I'm closing it."

Danny's on the porch. I'd told him to wait. I finish eating in record time, with Mom protesting the whole time while Danny patiently waits on the porch. I walk out.

"Let's go find Poindexter."

Danny looks puzzled. "Why?"

I sneer at him. "Why ask why, Danny? Just come on!"

We looked everywhere; in the park, at the store, even in the girls' locker room. Well, that last one was just for fun. Damned if he's not in the must unlikely place to find a kid in school. The dang library!

When we get to him, I take the right arm and Danny takes the left.

We carry him out feet dangling.

"Hey guys, what's up?"

Danny clings tighter. "You..."

The boy cries out, "Where you guys taking me? I can't be late for first hour."

I assure him, "You won't be."

Danny looks over at me. "What are we gonna do with this?"

Staring forward as we walk, I growl out, "I've got some questions for him and a gift. We'll take him behind the library, between the buildings."

Danny nods his head and says "OK."

When we get there, I turn to my partner. "You can go now, Danny."

"Why?" Danny asks again.

"Why ask why, man? We'll just catch up with you later."

He walks off like a wounded puppy with his tail between his legs.

Jack slams him against the wall again and yells. "What are you smiling for?" he asks.

Poindexter says. "Me? Oh no. No smile, not me."

Jack holds up the book bag. "What's this? And don't lie! I know you had it first."

It's my Spidey pack. He waves it in my face.

Jack is yelling again."What is this?"

Poindexter answers. "It's my Spidey pack."

Jack looks at the bag for a few seconds then shakes his head. "No, no, dummy!" He unzips the cool bag. Then he reaches in and pulls it out. "This?!"

Poindexter smiles: "Oh yeah, that." It's the diary.

Jack looks at his really big smile. Jack thinks. All I want to do is punch the little punk's teeth out. Man, does that smile piss me off.

Poindexter thinks Jack looks pissed. Maybe I shouldn't smile? So I stop, fast.

Suddenly Jack slams him against the wall again. "What are you smiling about?"

"Me? Oh no. No smile, not me."

Jack says again. "What is this? And don't lie!"

Poindexter looks down, and what do I tell him? He's got me. So I mumble "The book has your name on it, so I guess it's your diary?"

Jack opens the aged leather book. "I haven't written one word in it, but look--."

Poindexter looks real hard, but there is nothing. "What?"

Jack frantically thumbs through it, tearing every other page, but Poindexter still sees nothing in the book.

Jack is spluttering: "But, but there is nothing here..."

Jack begins to think, "Did I imagine the content? Was it in my head?" The book lies there in silence--not so much as a scratch as the diary's torn pages wave in the draft between the two buildings.

Jack has the book in one hand and Poindexter in the other.

Poindexter is thinking. There's not a thing I can say that will break the tension.

Jack is really lost. His grip loosens, and his mind is in another place. The anger is now washed away. His expressionless face looks completely numb. His face goes to the easiest expression for a face to handle: "But... but..." That is all he can say.

Poindexter asks, "Can I go now?" Putting both hands on the diary, Jack bent the soft cover. He stops even noticing me at all. I start to slowly walk away.

Jack yells, "Get back here. I'm not finished with you!"

Jack's loud command leaves my dangling foot hanging there in mid step. Dropping that foot would have been an act of war, so I draw my shoe back as if there's a big old snake lying underneath.

I look back. "But, Jack...," Poindexter starts to say.

Jack looks confused. "What *is* this? The diary talks to me. The dang thing even writes itself."

Poindexter looks down at the book. "It does?"

He tosses the brown leather thing in my hands. "Take this cursed book! I never want to see it again!"

Jack pushes me to the ground, then smiles with less confidence than I've seen from him before and says. "But if I do, you're dead!" Jack yells.

Jack stares down at him as Poindexter whimpers "But Jack..."

Jack grinds his teeth before saying. "No, just get rid of it." Poindexter looks angry. He glares at the cover, then looks up just in time to see Jack stroll away. Poindexter puts the diary in his bag, not knowing quite what to do. He goes to class.

Lunch is a bad one that day, a real gut-wrencher. Deep-fried mystery meat and corn bread that, as you eat it, makes you feel you're dehydrating. Water leaves your body taking refuge in the ten-day-old tree bark that the school calls corn bread. You tell yourself, "Chew, chew, chew," because the alternative is suffocation. But if you lived through that, the rest of the day was golden.

Poindexter's in the lunchroom with Ralph and Timmy. Timmy has just gotten out of the hospital. "I hear in the hospital you get all the ice cream you can eat," I say, as I'm eating my daily dose of poison.

"Yeah, it's cool, right?" At the same time he shifts uncomfortably in his chair. The little guy's hand is covering his side. Timmy's face is making all kinds of strange expressions, mainly painful ones.

"Are you OK, man?"

Timmy closes his eyes hard like. "Yeah, it's the stitches."

Simultaneously Ralph and I eagerly say, "Can I see?"

Timmy looks at us across the table with puppy dog eyes. His vulnerability makes me think about why I want to see his scar.

Ralph is a kid I only see in the lunchroom. We are the same age yet I have no classes with him. He is a big strong-looking guy with a Clark Kent demeanor to him, glasses and all. Stupid stuff comes out of his mouth all the time--he's a real live Clark Kent. Most kids run him off, but not us. We need all the friends we can get. You know, the whole United We Stand thing.

I'm having second thoughts about looking at a hole in someone, but Ralph is saying, "Come on, man. Let's see it."

Timmy shelters his bandage. "Mom told me to keep the bandage on."

Ralph leans forward. "She'll never know. Come on, man!"

I elbow Ralph. "He doesn't want to show us. Leave him alone!"

Ralph isn't letting up. "Don't be a wimp."

"I'm not a wimp, Clark!"

Ralph really hates it when we call him that. "Shut up, four eyes!"

"Both of you shut up!" I say.

The two of them glare at me. "It's bad enough I have to choke down this nasty lunchroom bile they call food. Now I have to listen to you mild cats. It's just too much!"

Ralph recoils. "Who died and made you lunchroom monitor?"

Timmy isn't saying anything, but I can tell he feels the same way. So I sit choking down what I can.

About five minutes later Timmy says "OK."

Ralph is driving his spoon into his stupid mouth over and over. He doesn't even pause. "OK what?" His mouth is still full.

Timmy stares over at us. "OK, you can see."

Ralph drops the spoon. "Really?"

Timmy lifts his shirt and pulls the large bandage away from his skin.

"Hurry before I change my mind!"

I jump up and look. "Oh, sick! It looks like the doctor screwed up." The three-inch hole has about thirty stitches over it, stitches holding stitches. The jagged hole looks like a chain saw got hold of him.

Ralph squints his eyes and whips his head back away in disgust. "Yeah, man, that's gross!"

Timmy pulls his shirt down. "The doctor didn't do that. Jack did!" He gets even more serious. He stops and peers down. "Jack is a real jerk," he quickly mumbles as he surveys the room. We quietly agree.

I clench my bag. "How did Jack do that?"

"Well, don't tell anyone, but..."

He tells us a story about Jack starting a fire in the bathroom and splitting his stitches open with one shot to the gut. The book isn't helping at all! I begin to tell them about the diary.

Ralph smiles sarcastically. "Boy, did that Indian guy take you for a ride?" Then he says, "Let's see it."

"See what?"

"The book, dummy!"

Timmy is eager to get off the topic of himself. "Yeah," he says.

I reach into my bag and begin to dig. In my backpack there are papers, schoolbooks and all kinds of things, but no diary. It's gone!

VII
JACK'S D DAY

Now that all is well in Hellville, I think I can get back to Jack duties. I start by taking a kid's math homework.

"Jack, I worked hours on that!"

"Well, good. I expect an A then."

I erase his name, Samuel, and put mine in. I hate algebra anyway.

He says. "You're a jerk, Jack!" as I walk away.

I flip back around. His eyes open up kind of like Gollum in the Lord of the Rings. His peepers are two big gray pools of fear. As I walk back in his direction, he shuffles off down the hallway in his oversized wrinkled-up old blue jeans. He scoots through the crowd. I jog up to the people that he slides past. They're all staring at me. I yell, "What are you looking at?" They stare back and say nothing.

I repeat, "What are you looking at?" The crowd slowly breaks up. I smile and I'm turning around when my nose suddenly explodes and I stumble backward. All I see is red. The palm of my hand slams against the locker before my back. I ooze down the locker, like chocolate pudding on a white wall.

I lay there with my hands cupping my nose, trying to figure out what happened, when a loud voice yells, "How's it hanging Jack?"

I don't quite know how to answer, and I'm confused because I can't tell if tears are running off my hands or if it's blood. My face feels like a furnace and my vision is still in quietus.

The calm voice says, "Now Jack it's rude to ignore someone when they're talking to you. Didn't anyone teach you any manners?"

I whimper "Aaah—aaah."

The calm voice goes dark and the volume goes way up. "Look at people when they're talking to you, boy!"

The red is almost gone now, but my hands don't want to leave my face for fear of another assault. I don't think I've ever been hit this hard before.

Slowly I peeled my hands free from my face. The crowd is now in a circle around me in the hallway. I can see people standing in the back row jumping up and down to view my demise. Right in front of me are three guys in letter jackets. That's kind of strange because it's 90 degrees outside.

We don't get to see many high-school letter jackets on any day here. My Dad has one hanging up in the hallway of our house. But these guys don't have as many pins hanging off their jackets.

The smaller one in the middle--damned if it isn't Iron Skull--says, "Now that's better. I'm only going to tell you one time. Only once."

Just then Barbie walks out from between them and smiles. "I told you Jack," she simpers. Iron Skull pushes her back behind him. His voice gets louder. "Jack, Jack, Jack, if you ever touch her again, well, here, let me help you." He reaches down to pull me up. I stick my hand out, only to see blood. We lock hands, and he pulls me off the ground, but in the same motion he rushes towards me and socks me in the gut. I double over as the huge bodyguards grab each arm to keep me from going back down.

Iron Skull smiles as he pushes my head back. "Do you understand, my friend?" In between coughs I cry out, "Yes, yes, I do."

In the background you can hear, "Hit him again! Hit him again!" After a while it sounds like the whole school chanting, "Hit 'm! Hit 'm! Hit 'm!"

Iron Skull looks around as he grabs a tuft of my hair and pulls my head back. He gets real close and wipes my blood from his hand onto my shirt, first the front then the back, real casual like. "They don't like you much. Do they?"

I think I even heard a teacher chant "Hit 'm." Off to the side I could see Danny waiting to pounce, but he looked at the three real slow and then backed into the crowd out of sight. I think to myself, "What a coward he is! My best chance of getting out of here, and now he's gone."

Iron skull snaps his fingers. "Wake up, Jack! I'm not through with you yet." He smiles. "How did you get so many friends there, Jack?"

I looked him in the eyes. "Just lucky I guess."

He nailed me again. The crowd roars. "Now, Jack, don't be sarcastic." His smile leaves. "Is this funny to you?"

I look him in the eyes in defiance. "No, man. This isn't funny." I'm getting an idea of just how bad it feels to be picked on. No one has ever treated me like this before. Come to think of it, this is the first time I've ever been on the ugly end of a fight. I'm saying something I never thought I would ever say:

"Please man, let me go. I'm sorry. I'll never do it again, I promise."

The biggest guy pokes me in the chest with his free hand and says, "You dang-right you won't."

I can see the silhouette of Barbie moving back and forth, looking out from behind the quarterback. "You're not going to pick on me anymore, Jack!" she crows.

She was right about that. Her boyfriend puts his arm in front of her and says abruptly, "Now shut up, Tina."

She hits him in the chest. "Daddy never lets anyone talk to me like that! Who do you think you are?"

His voice goes soft. "Now, baby…"

She starts to stomp away. "Don't you baby me!"

He cowers off behind her. "But, baby…"

The two linemen let go of my arms. I crumple again to the floor.

They push a hole in the crowd and lumber off behind Iron Skull.

On all fours, I look up at the same people that were scared of me minutes ago. But my armor, their fear, has been taken from me. They're no longer afraid.

I cry out, "What are you looking at?" But this time they laugh, and just stare at me.

VIII
END GAME

Walking home was takes forever, though I often brag about how close my home is to school. The bleeding has stopped, but my white shirt is covered with blood all across my chest. It sticks to my skin, and my ears won't stop ringing. When I put my feet down, it feels like little explosions in my head.

When I get home, I see through the plate glass window Mom vacuuming the living room. So I sneak around the side of the house to my bedroom. The wood frame around my window has been broken for quite some time, so I jimmy the window up and begin to crawl inside onto my bed, which is right inside the window. Then someone grabs the back of my belt and jerks me back out of the window frame. Part of the wooden window disintegrates in my hands. I look behind me and see Danny. With one motion, I flip around and elbow Danny on the side of the neck.

I walk towards him as he backs up.

"What are you doing here?"

His face goes all puppy dog. "Man, I just came to see if you're OK. You look like crap, man."

I yell, "Why didn't you help me, coward?" I push him.

"Help you?"

"Yeah, help me!"

He put his hands out to stop me from pushing him again.

"Man, if I would have tried to help you, they would've kicked my ass too!"

"What kind of friend are you, Danny?"

He pokes me in the chest with an angry look on his face.

"I'm the ONLY friend you've got, Jack!"

He's right. Danny is the only friend I have. I say nothing as I walk around him and crawl back into my bedroom window. He keeps calling my name. I just close my window, peel off my T-shirt and lie there in bed. I quickly go to sleep. I begin to dream about running from Iron Skull and his posse. I'm running as hard as my feet will carry me. My feet feel like real heavy lead bars, I strain to make each step. I'm moving in slow motion, but the world around me isn't. I'm in a dark neighborhood, and in that neighborhood are dark houses with even darker windows. I'm running down the street towards a bright light. Iron Skull and his big friends are in my shadow. They squint their eyes as they look into the light I'm running towards.

The light gets brighter and brighter as we get closer, until it finally surrounds me. Iron Skull is no longer following me, I feel like I'm in a place he cannot come. Not a private place but a safe place. I walk through a crowd of people smiling at me. They seem to be happy to see me. These people aren't angry about something I have done. They're not watching my every move to make sure I'm not doing something wrong. I begin to smile, feeling happy.

Now everything around me is in slow motion except me. People are slowly patting me on the back. That I'm not moving in slow motion makes it excruciatingly difficult, because I have to wait for their hands to touch me. No one has ever patted me on the back and said, "Good job, Jack... You're a good kid." But as long as I stand here and wait, these people do that.

I'm not used to this love and friendship; it's stinging my skin, like the switch Pop uses on me. But it feels so good inside to have people actually like me. I can't move away. I won't move away! People actually like me.

"Jack!" I'm being shaken awake.

Dad yells again. "Jack!"

"Dad...?" My eyes open.

"What's wrong?" I say to him. He looks pissed.

"You know what's wrong!"

It could be one of many things or nothing at all. But looking at Dad's angry face, it's something all right.

"What's this, boy?" He lifts up the diary.

I point at it with my whole hand, almost grabbing the book.

I say to him, "How did...?" He cuts me off with a swat on the head with the diary.

He points the rolled-up thing at my face. "Don't say another word!"

"Yes, sir." Oops...it just slipped out.

He tightens his fist around the brown cover. "Do you think I'm joking? Is this funny to you?"

Then Dad opens the diary and begins to read: "Dad can't find out but I stole a kid's milk money and beat the boy up. After that I took Ms. Hillbloom's apples..."

"What is this? Watergate?"

Dad pauses and looks at me like he wants me to talk.
I'm just stunned, so I can't say anything. I just wish I was still asleep.

Dad looks down at me. "Well, President Nixon, I guess you wish you didn't write this down?"

I don't understand what he's talking about, but he's right about one thing. I do wish that I had never seen that damn diary my whole life!

"Boy, this goes on and on. Why the heck did you write this down? Is this your way of turning yourself in?"

I think to myself, "No way, man!" I couldn't believe this was happening. If I tell Dad about the book, the old man might find me a straitjacket and two big fellows in white coats to put it on. So, I just give him a dumb look. Kind of like Barney gives all those little kids.

"You've got a lot of apologizing to do, and for your punishment I'd beat you, but by the look of it someone's already done that. So, we'll go with as much work as I can find for you."

"But Dad?"

Dad wipes the sweat from his face. "So, it talks," he says, referring to me, his son.

I open my mouth again, but what comes out makes no sense. The blood crusted around my nose hurts while I try to talk.

What I'm saying must sound like. "Blo Ba Bloo, Ba Bloo Bloo Bloo."

He puts his index finger over his mouth. "Shhhh, boy. We start work at 7:00 A.M. sharp. So get plenty of sleep. I'm going to work you till the sun goes down!"

I look at the clock across my room. Its only 3:00 P.M. Dad never gets home this early. Two hours is enough time to work some employee to death or erect the Sistine Chapel. He walks towards the door, then out. He still has the book in his hand. As the door is shutting, Dad slowly turns around. "And clean your face. You look like hell," he says.

Cleaning crusted blood out of your nose isn't easy. The blood is hanging on like a booger with blades. It is still light outside, but I'm in a hurry to get back to my dreams.

I know it all started when the book showed up. So if I can somehow give the diary back, this will all stop, maybe. I decide to go and get rid of the diary. I go out the same way I came in, the window. Dad is unloading his old Chevy Ford. I call it that 'cause the funny thing has more personality than any car on the road. First of all, the truck has a light green passenger-side door, but the body is blue. The hood is rust brown with a tarnished silver Ford sign right in front. The driver-side door is caved in so bad the window won't roll down. The kicker is that the bed of this truck is brown, and if you walk to the back, the tailgate says Chevy on it.

He gets his truck unloaded. Then the old man throws his yellow work gloves on the bench seat along with my diary. As the book flies out of Dad's hand, I can tell he's disappointed in me just by the look on his face.

I get the diary out of the truck and go to Poindexter's house to give it to him, or at least get rid of it forever. His mom answers the door. I open my mouth to ask if the boy is home, but I realize I don't even know his real name. His mom stares me down as we stand there in muted silence. I can't even hear the birds or the crickets. The wind has even stopped. I think for a minute.

Well, I can't just call him Poindexter. Maybe I can guess his name. Maybe He's a Harry or Bob. No, no, he looks more like a Simon. So I just say, "Is your son here?" His mom smirks at me. I try to say something, but she puts her hand up to tell me just to shut up. She says, "Hold on" and closes the metal screen door. She's on her way back into the house. Seconds later Poindexter walks up and stands inside the door. Thank god. He puts his hands flat on the screen.

I turn around and wave him outside. "Come here," I say. His eyes bug out. "You're not gonna hit me, are ya?" he demands.

"No, man. Get out here!"

He slowly comes out from behind the creaking door and asks, "What's wrong?"

I look him dead in the eyes. "You know what's wrong!" I say. I slap the book in his hand and step back. "How do we get rid of this?" I demand. The boy says, "We? What do you mean 'we'?" I pull my fist back, the book rumbles, shaking the boy's hand as if in direct protest of my action.

POINDEXTER flinches and throws my arms up to block Jack's blow, pausing there for a few seconds. It feels like Jack is trying to pull the book outta my hand, but the blow never comes. I peep out and see Jack holding himself back. The book seems to be moving on its own, like there's a live animal inside or something tied to it. I drop the diary onto the wooden porch planks and step back till my front door stops me. Jack is jumping around. "See, see, this thing is crazy. How do WE get rid of this thing?" he says. I look up from the diary at Jack and say, "I don't know how you get rid of this!" Then Jack walks up and grabs the diary.

JACK doesn't seem to be listening to me, but this boy's gonna help me whether he likes it or not. I grab his arm and plant the diary in his hand again. "Now hold onto this!" I tell him.

POINDEXTER keeps telling him I don't know how to get rid of the book. Finally, Jack rubs his head and asks, "Where did you get this book?"

I hesitate for a second or two, then answer, "Over on East Main, in the old addition, at an Indian herb shop."

Jack grabs my arm and pulls me off the porch. Before I know it, we're at the bus stop three blocks away. His hand never loosens until we stop. "I can't go to the bookstore," I tell him. "I've got homework and I have to eat dinner. Mom hates it when I'm late." Jack flips around and grabs the back of my head; he towers over me. "Trust me, you're gonna be late tonight!" The crosstown bus arrives right on time. Jack pushes me on and then asks, "You have any money?" I reach into my left pocket and feel nothing. I hand the book to Jack.

Jack hands me the book and pulls out a dollar bill. The bus driver tells us, "It's sixty-five cents apiece boys." The boy shrugs his shoulders to tell me he has no more. I reach in my left-hand pocket and feel nothing but lint. So I drop the book in the bus driver's hand.

THE OLD BUS DRIVER SAYS: Don't this boy know I ain't no book rack? I let the book drop to my lap. Bein' a bus driver sucks bad 'nough. Why ain't these kids never has their money ready? Everybody has to wait for these little brats. So I says, "You needs to have your money ready before you get on the bus. This ain't your own personal taxi!" That bigger boy who seems to be in charge finally tugs out of his pocket the rest of the money. They walk back to their seats and sit down.

I kept peering back at them two. The scrawny feller looks more and more worried the farther we get along. But the big fella even looks like he has him somethin' serious to do. Them boys is talking all serious like. I's been on the job going on for 20 years, and if it were up to my wife, I be on the job for 20 more. I don't seem to be able to take my minds off them kids. They reminds me of my own, clueless as to what's out there in the world.

So I says to them, "Where you boys goin' in such a hurry?"

I look them back in my mirror, waiting for an answer. The little one jumps up first and says, "We're going to East Main!"

"You boys shouldn't be off in those parts. Them area's dangerous!"

The big fella look at me like I ought to mind my own business, so I take the hint and drive on. We arrive at their destination. They file off disorganized like. As they step off the bus, I says, "You boys be careful now!" Then that stinkin' book begins to jump up and down in my lap. It scares me a little bit. Just as the door is shutting, I sling the book out to them.

Jack picks up the book and hits the boy in the chest with it. I tell him, "Keep hold of this thing till we give the thing back." He says, "I don't want to carry it!" I say, "I didn't ask you to carry the book. I'm TELLING you to carry it!" On the bus he had told me about the Indian guy and how he got the book.

POINDEXTER reaches out and grabs it as Jack lets go. I lead him towards the shop. Just as we arrive, the Indian man comes to the door like he was expecting us. "Oh, Young Sir, I've been expecting you! And you brought a guest along too!" Jack rips the book away from me and waves it in the face of the Indian guy.

JACK is trying to give him back the diary. Meanwhile, I'm yelling "What is this?!"

The strange-looking guy brings his hand up. His eyes begin to quiver. The book is working its way out of my hand. Scared, I peer over at the boy out of the corner of my eye. He looks at ease, but that doesn't calm me, and I can't hold on to the book any more.

POINDEXTER sees the man raise his hand and the book flies free from Jack. It levitates in one spot at eye level. Jack tumbles back and I cross my arms. I look in amazement as Jack winces. The book pulsates as if each page is sucking in air. Then the book begins to talk: "You can't escape, Jack. Not even the Creator can save you now."

The Indian fella's eyes are rolled back in his head, and he's waving back and forth like a reed in the wind. My smile vanishes. What did I get Jack into? Jack stands without words or expression. I've tossed him to the dogs, and the book is shearing Jack's spirit away.

All of a sudden, the book begins to speak: "Be it a twist of fate, or an act of chance, we— yes, you and I--have been thrust together. Until you change, I will always be by your side."

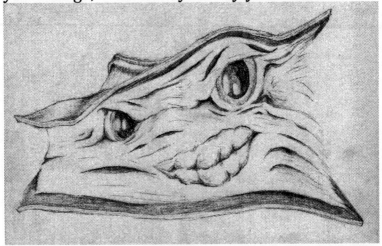

Tears roll out of Jack's eyes. He cries out, "Please, how can I end this? You've won." The book dims and slowly lowers to chest level. "Start by being nice to others, and that can show in your actions, not only in your words." The light disappears into each page as it lowers into Jack's hands. The Indian guy comes back to life. JACK: The guy looks real tired all the sudden. He's holding himself up with a glass countertop. He says, "Young Sirs, our time has come to an end, but we shall meet another day." He pushes us out the door and turns the "Open" sign to "Closed." He turns the blinds till I can't see him anymore.

On our way home I toss the diary out the window into the lake. The boy stops and watches me walk away. He asks, "What are you doing, Jack?"

I say, "Trust me. It'll find its way home."

POINDEXTER starts to walk behind Jack. "Well, I guess you're right about that jack," I tell him.

IX
APOLOGY ACCEPTED

Mom is waking me up. It's 6:00 in the morning. I know that because she keeps saying it over and over again.

"Honey, it's 6:00. It's time to get up."

"Mom, can't I sleep a little longer?" I put my pillow over my head to cover my ears so I can't hear her say no.

Sure enough she says, "No, honey, it's time to get up."

Doesn't take a genius to know what I say next.

"But Mom!"

Mom pulls the pillow away from me and says, "Your breakfast is getting cold."

Then Mom pulls the blankets off onto the floor. A chill comes over me. It isn't like the room's cold or even cool; it's just a sudden change of temperature that snaps me out of my slumber. The feeling is like jumping into cold water or snow trickling down your back.

So I put on my work clothes and begin to go to the dining room. But I remember the work boots that Dad bought for me are under my bed. I reach under to feel my box with all my money in it, I now have enough money to buy my air rifle, but I know if I get it, that damn book will tell on me.

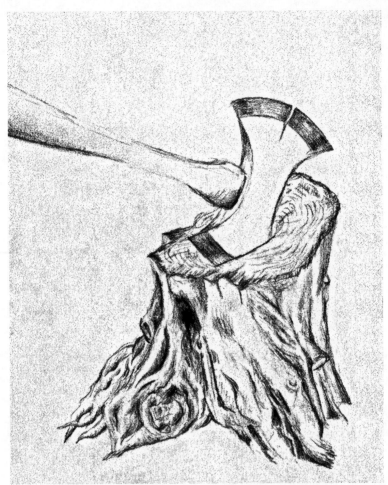

As I'm getting in Dad's old work truck, I see it. The book appears as though the thing had never moved. I act like it isn't even there. I turn to shut my door. When the metal door slams, it always makes a deep sound that if you heard it at any other time, you would think something just broke or somebody just made a big mistake.

I get my fingers caught in the door one time. They disappear into the crack as if I am shaking hands with Dad's truck. You know when you're shaking hands with Grandpa and he turns your bones into powdered milk. Well that's just mild compared to what Dad's door can do to you. My hand throbs for days after that.

Well, I'm in the belly of the beast now, rolling down the Hillbloom Drive. Dad's multicolored truck careens down the road like it has lead tires and rock shocks. Most vehicles roll over bumps in the road smoothly, but Dad's truck crashes into them. Every bump is a collision that shakes the teeth even of people walking on the sidewalk.

We arrive on-site and Dad happily points to a pile of wood as one of his workers backs a trailer next to it. "Well, get to work, son. It ain't goin' to get done without ya." I jump out and slam the door behind me. I begin slinging wood into the wooden-railed trailer. Every time I take a little break, Dad comes down on me like a ton of bricks.

"What do you think this is? A spa for lazy kids. I'll tell you when you can take a break."

I think to myself, "This is more like a prison camp for the joy of abusive fathers." But I just say, "Dad, I'm tired!"

He reaches into his back pocket and pulls out the diary. He begins to read to his workers up on the scaffolding. "Listen to this, guys: 'As I was going into the school, I pulled two girls' hair. As if that wasn't enough, I punched a boy in the gut, then...' He wrote this, it's in his handwriting, and that's not all: The book is full of this crap!"

He begins to read again: "Then I caught the trash can on fire."

He lowers the book in disgust, then folds it. He looks back up at his workers.

"I wouldn't have believed it if I didn't read in the newspaper about the school janitor who burned his hands putting out a trash-can fire a few days ago."

The two workers look at me as if I'm Public Enemy No. 1. Their expression puts Dad's hands in the air. He asks them, "What would you guys do?"

The toothless old man yells out. "I'd tan that boy's hide!"

The super thin worker named Delbert looks down at me from the scaffolding, you know the guy with the BB gun. "Well," he says, "You wrote that?"

I look up to him and say nothing.

He shakes his head and says, "Man, that was stupid..."

Dad yells, "All of you get back to work! I'm not paying you to stand around."

"He's not paying me anyway..." I mumble.

Lunch hits right at noon. That doesn't always happen. If Dad feels like working through lunch, well, that's just what happens. You never hear any complaints from Dad's workers. Most workers barely last a day, but these two are gluttons for punishment. I'm sitting underneath a tree on a well-groomed lawn eating what Mom made for me. Delbert walks up and sits next to me.

"Well, did you get the money?"

I take a bite of my sandwich. Delbert reaches into my lunch sack to grab a handful of grapes. He says, "You know someone else is interested in the gun. He offered me more money, but I like you, so I told him no way. But if you don't get it soon, I'll have to sell it to him." Delbert's greasy hair brushes across my arm. I recoil, and I tell him, "I can't buy your gun."

Delbert looks at me in surprise. He says quickly. "Why not?"

I yell out, "I just can't!"

Hey man, I've been waiting months for you to get money together. What's your problem?" His face goes pissed.

"I, I, just can't!"

I roll my bag up and begin to walk away. Delbert grabs my arm. I flip around. He looks me in the eye. "That's cool, man..." He gives me a big old smile. "Is it the money? Maybe I can knock off 25 bucks..."

I pull my hand free and walk.

"OK, 50!" he exclaims.

"I just can't," I tell him again.

The rest of the day just grinds along. Delbert glares at me every chance he gets. Dad kept his word: the sun was down when we were finally going home.

X

TELL NO LIES

I have a big one that not even the book has talked about, a real doozy. I'm going to tell you now about it. The time is right. But if I tell you, none of you will like me. It's not like I killed the neighbor's cat or pulled the plug on Mother Teresa, but it's pretty bad. Well, let's see... It all started on a...

Forget it! You guys aren't ready for this anyway.

Sunday morning, my soft pillow has a familiar bulge beneath it. I reach in between my sheets to grab what seems to be a mad porcupine. The angry animal's quills jab into my digits hard and fast. The pillow flies off the bed and onto the floor. The diary slowly floats higher and higher. My name is glowing right off the cover brighter and brighter, higher and higher; it's as bright as the sun and high too.

The voice comes out from the light. "Jack, Jack, Jack, are you going to be good now?" Every time the voice says a word the light blows up so bright that my pupils are getting a suntan.

I cover my eyes and ask "Why are you doing this to me?"

The light from the book strobes along with every word it speaks: "Jack, who told you that it's OK to answer a question with a question?"

I peer out from the covers.

"What?"

"Well, Jack, it's time..."

I interrupt: "Time for what?"

The light goes to a pure white. "Time for you to listen!"

The light is right. It is time to listen. My face relaxes because I can't fight this thing anymore. Some people never change. They start out on a path--good or bad--and that's it. I've never met such a thing that just can't be beaten. At every turn the diary is right there to meet me. Yeah, I know I'm being a wimp, but it just won't stop.

"It's time. Well, what will I do?"

The book moves towards me. "Saying you're sorry would be a good start."

I think out loud. "Who do I need to apologize to?"

The light flutters. "Jack, who do you NOT need to apologize to?" The diary ripples like it's in a pool of water. "If you didn't need to apologize to everyone you've ever met, I wouldn't need to be here, would I? Oh, and give the money"

Jack cries out. "NO!"

The book goes cool and drops back to my bed.

That evening after work I walk into the kitchen. I'm so tired from digging this huge ditch that I don't even think Dad needs. Or maybe it is my fear of admitting I'm wrong to everyone. I'm holding my head down and thinking about what the hell...I mean, what the heck am I'm going to change about myself?

Mom peeks out from behind the refrigerator door and says, "Are you hungry, sweetie?"

I jump back in surprise. I mumble "No, thanks!" I'm really hungry, but she scared the crap out of me.

I guess Mom heard me. She smiles and says, "Are you sure? I made cookies, and there's cold milk right in here." She points into the fridge.

"Yes, please."

Her happy face shows even more joy. Mom's in total shock. After a few minutes she comes out of it. "You just said 'thanks' and 'please.' My boy's growing up." She repeats that a couple of times, as she kisses and hugs me over and over again.

This is a good start.

It's Monday morning. Hitting and chasing kids has lost its luster. The pre-summer trees are shaking their dark green leaves in the wind. They sound like thousands of people clapping for me.

Heading through the park, I see Danny. He's holding up Poindexter.

I can hear him saying, "Give me the money!" He's shaking the boy like a rag doll.

The boy quietly says, "OK."

I run up and yell, "Give the kid a break."

"What? Do you want some of this?"
He holds Poindexter out for me to take
over.

"No Danny, it's time." I pull Danny's
hands off the boy's shirt.

"It's time? What the hell are you
talking about, Jack?!" Danny steps back.
Poindexter to my surprise doesn't run off.
He just stands there stunned.

"Are you OK, man?" Danny just can't
believe hearing me ask it.

Poindexter with his mouth wide open
says, "Yeah, are you OK, man?"

I curl my brow and say, "Shut up,
Poindexter!"

Poindexter screams at the top of his
lungs, "WHY do you keep calling me that?
My name is..."

Danny thumps Poindexter in the chest.
It stops him cold. Danny yells, "No one
cares what your stupid name is!"

I stare Danny down. "Leave the kid
alone!" I tell him.

"Jack, let's go steal something or beat
some kid up. Let's have some fun. Come on,
Jack."

It just doesn't sound like fun anymore. More like a hassle. "No, man. I can't do that stuff anymore."

"Why not?" Danny asks.

"Yeah, why not?" Poindexter wants to know.

I peer down at Poindexter. He says, "OK, OK, I'll shut up!"

"It can't be me anymore. Those things are wrong. I'm sorry I made you do all those bad things for so long."

Danny crosses him arms and says, "You didn't make me do anything. I do what I want!"

I put my hand on Danny's shoulder. "I didn't realize how many people I hurt."

Danny wants to know, "What happen to 'Let's get ours'?"

I reach in to my pocket and pull all the money I took from him to put it in his hands. "What we're taking from others isn't ours, Danny. It just isn't right."

He throws my arm off. "You're crazy, man. I'm outta here!"

Danny walks away. I don't know if I believe all that stuff I said or not, but I'm sticking with it for now. Poindexter is stunned so I put my hand on his shoulder and head for school.

Soon word about my changes is getting around. By lunch people who ran from me are walking up and poking fun at me, like I'm a circus animal or something. I'm starting to think, it ain't easy being good.

But I take it. Dad had told me to be home right after school. Nowadays Dad only threatens to bring the paddle out because I can foresee Dad snapping and just forgetting to stop. Then, if he finally stops, there will be a puddle of Jack at the end of his paddle.

I run in the front door. I yell, "I'm home," but no one answers.

I walk into the kitchen. Mom, Dad-- and to my surprise--Poindexter's Mom are sitting there. "Is everything OK?" I ask. I know I'm going down in flames. I just know it.

Dad speaks first. "This lady--." Dad looks real embarrassed. "I'm sorry. I mean,

Ms. Jones said you helped her kid out. Is that true?"

Mom leans forward. "What your father means is, Did you save Ms. Jones son from getting beat up?"

I thought about telling them that Poindexter almost gets beat up every day. Yes, even by yours truly. But I didn't. I just say "Yes."

Mom gives me that goofy smile. "I knew something changed in you! I knew it."

Dad scratches his head without really scratching. You know, he gives me that why-the-heck-did-you-do-that? look.
Poindexter's Mom jumps up and gives me an I-only-see-you-once-a-year grandma hug. She tells me, "Thank you. Thank you. Since my husband passed away, my baby hasn't had any friends, not one."

The lady calls Poindexter BABY! What a dork. And she kept going:

"He never talks about school or anything. You're a godsend."

I try and play it out. "Lady, I mean Ms. Jones, it's not that big of a deal."

"But it IS. For what you did I'm going to take you to Springfield amusement park this weekend."

"Sorry, ma'am, he's being punished this weekend," Dad interrupts.

Mom covers Dad's hands with hers. "Honey, can't we talk about this?"

Dad looks over at Mom. "He needs..."

Mom pats his hands and tells the lady. "We'll talk." The lady gives an understanding smile.

After the lady goes home Dad takes me on a road trip.

In the truck on the way he turns to me and says, "What happened to the diary?" I shifted in my seat and tell him, "It came back to me. I mean, I got it back."

He looks at me a little longer than he should. We almost run off the road. "You didn't write that stuff, did you?"

I look Dad square in the eyes. "No, Dad, I didn't."

"But you did those things, didn't you?"

"Yes, Dad, I did." I can't lie to him anymore.

Dad looks real serious. "I forgot, but when I was about your age I was on the wrong path. Doing mean stuff to everyone, and just being an all around jerk. It was so easy, everything I wanted I stole it. If I didn't like someone I beat them up. Till one day an Indian guy gave me this book, it even had my name on it. The book changed me too."

"You too?"

"Yeah, me too." He pauses as we turn and drive up a long driveway. Dad smiles. He almost never did that so it really put me off a bit. He says, "I guess it's time to clean up your mess."

"I don't understand, Dad," I tell him. But just as I got the last word out, we drive around a clump of trees. I see Ms. Hillbloom's house.

I know what to do. So I get out of Dad's truck looking back at him as I walk up to Hillbloom Manor and knock on the enormous wooden door. Time had done its worst to the majestic entryway, but bam, bam, bam, I knock real hard on the door. She's taking her time to get to the door, but I'm waiting.

The handle twists and the door creaks open.

Old Lady Hillbloom stands in the doorway. "Do I know you? Do I?" she asks.

I look across at her. She's not so tall or scary. "No, ma'am."

"Well, go away then!" She starts to close the door.

I say to her before she closes the door, "I'm sorry for...!" She begins to open the door back up and looks right at me. "Why are you sorry?"

Now the hard part: "I was the one who broke your window and stole your apples."

She moves towards me. "Do you know how precious this house is to me?" she wants to know.

I lower my head. "No, ma'am."

Ms. Hillbloom moves out onto the rock porch. "The house is the only thing I have left from Roger," she tells me again.

"Yes, ma'am." I hear Dad getting out of the truck.

"This house is all I have left. Roger built all these houses." She waves her hand across the whole town.

Dad comes up and says, "He's going to fix it. I mean, we're going to fix it."

Dad loses patience with Ms. Hillbloom and he begins to walk, so we follow him around her house, looking at all the damage time did. Rocks barely hanging on, like a baby tooth holding to a thread of skin. Cracks in walls are streaming into the ground. Gutters have rusted through from relentless rains that started long before I was born.

"Your home is beautiful, Ms.--" Dad looks down at me.
I open my mouth to say, "Are you looking at the same house I am?" but before I could say a word, Dad shushes me.
She stops in the backyard and looks up at her house.

The next day we've worked the whole time tearing wood from the window and cleaning the yard. The old lady is nowhere to be found. The new window is real heavy. Dad asks me to hold the massive thing from the inside. I'm holding it in the hole with all I've got while Pop hammers it into place. Then I begin to hear it in the background, the lowest notes on a piano. So I turn to hear it better.

The sound is familiar. It goes like this: There are four fast poundings of the keyboard: Dum, dum, dum, dum. And then four faster notes: dum, dum, dum, dum. Then it's even faster than before: Dum, dum, dum, dum. And the whole thing starts over again. Those four repetitive notes give me an eerie feeling, so I back up to the window and slide my hands in the gap. I try to pull the window up. Dad yells, "Go around."

I protest, "But, Dad..."

He points his hammer at me. "Go around!"

Slowly I walk away from the window into the room. The door inside has big, thick metal bands across it. I'm slowly creeping through the next room. There are curtains floating in the wind, but I can't really feel the wind. The hallway has old pictures of people in big ties and long hair. These guys have skinny mustaches that come to a tiny little point like a needle. They all look like these guys won something, like a war or something.

The walls are light brown or aged white, I think. The wood floors are creaking as if no one has walked on them for years. Some parts of the walls have exposed wood slats. I run my hand across the hallway table as I walk by, a layer of dust rolls off. It feels like I put my hand in a sand box, the dust is so thick.

Queak, queak. The rug quiets it down but you can still hear the noise. Branches are woven into the design of the rug, pointing me forward as if to tell me to keep going. My reluctant footsteps slowly shuffle on the rug's open threads. The rug is flowing to the end of the long hall and turns to the stairwell.

You think the hall is loud. The stairs sound like they are going to snap apart. I put my butt cheek on the banister to slide down. As I come to the end, out comes Ms. Hillbloom right in front of me.

Loudly she says, "What do you think you are doing?"

I can't stop sliding down. "I, I'm sorry..." Thump! I hit the post at the bottom and fly off onto the ground, rolling and bouncing to a stop. At the end of my painful journey I bump a stand with a big old vase on it. The blue and white thing looks like it costs more than I'm worth. And to my horror, it's rocking back and forth. I jump up to catch it, but I'm too late. Crash! It hits the ground and breaks into a million pieces. Ms. Hillbloom and I look at each other for what feels like an incredibly long time.

She scratches her head and says, "Well, I hated that piece anyway."

Ms. Hillbloom bends over to pull me up. I reach out, and she gives me her hand.

"You have lots of energy, don't you?" she observes.

I stand here, not knowing quite what to say.

"What? Is there no air in you belly?"

I crinkle my brows. "What did you say?"

"Boy, don't you know what air in your belly means?" She pats me on the breadbasket. "OK, how about cat got your tongue?"

I put my hand on the top of my head. "Oh, cat got my tongue...I got it. Now what was the question?"

Ms. Hillbloom gives me a blank stare.

We walk into her living room where the noises came from. In the middle of the room is a shiny black piano. This shiny thing is polished in a room full of dust. It's as if the piano is the only thing that matters. A hinged wing shoots out of the top, the only thing holding it up is a long thin stick. I can see a guy in a black tux sitting down in front of this thing to play classical music.

Ms. Hillbloom sits down and begins to play Bach
or Beethoven, real ear wrenchers. She sits on the bench and pats it with the palm of her hand. What I think she is trying to do is to get me to sit down next to her. "Come here," Old Lady Hillbloom says.

I slowly walk over to her. She looks up at me and smiles.

"Have you ever played?"

"Played on one of these?"

She rubs the black wood. "Yes?"

"Only to pretend." I slap my hands across the keys. Ugly sounds cry out. The old lady puts her fingers over mine. I stop. She presses one digit, then another. She moves my hand over the keys, and as she presses, music comes out. It begins to make sense. The sounds are starting to be familiar. I'd say it sounds good, but heck, it's only my first time. I can't help but smile.

She says, "Your long fingers are like many great pianists'."

I look down as I flip my hands in front of my face. "They are?" I say.

She cups my hands and tells me, "Talent is but hard work."

Not knowing if I can believe her, I reluctantly reply, "It is?"

"The great piano players of the world started right here."

I look around. "In this room?"

She smiles real big. "No, but on a bench just like this one. In front of a piano just like you are."

I turn my head to look at her. "Do you think I can be great?"

"Maybe, if you work real hard."

"How can I start?"

"You just did."

We work for hours. Well, it feels like hours. Dad walks in. "Where have you been?" Dad says to me. "He hasn't been bothering you, ma'am, has he?" he says to her.

"No, the young man is delightful."

Dad looks surprised, "He is?"

She grabs my hand. "This young man has the hands of a pianist."

Dad's expression doesn't change. "He does?"

She looks annoyed. "Yes, this young man does have talent! Bring the boy up here every day after school to learn the art of the great pianist!"

To help Dad understand, I say, "Dad, listen" and try to play something, but the sounds are horrible.

But he says, "Great. Come on, boy."

Ms. Hillbloom exclaims, "I mean it. You need to bring him every day after school so I can train him!"

"But I, I can't!" I say.

Dad shrugs his shoulders. "No, he can't," he agrees.

Ms. Hillbloom stands up. She has an angry look.

"Just because you missed your calling doesn't imply you should make the boy miss his."

"We can't afford to pay you for my boy's lessons."

Then she smiles and says, "It, of course, is gratis."

Dad looks at her like he knows what the old lady is saying. "Yes, I know it is expensive."

Her smile intensifies. "No my boy, it's pro bono."

By the look on Dad's face, he still has no idea what the old lady is saying. I can't say much. I have no idea either.

She slowly shakes her head like she is annoyed by him.

"It's FREE."

Dad smiles back to her. "Ooooh, free..."

We both understand that word. I thought, "Why the heck didn't she say that in the first place?"

Dad comes out of it, and he looks serious again.

"First of all, he doesn't have time to come here and play. He is being punished. And the boy needs to learn how to make money too. He is never gonna be..."

She cuts him off. "Little William, you had problems too..." Ms. Hillbloom glares at Dad for quite a while. "Just like your troubled offspring."

Dad points his face at the ground and quietly says, "Yes, ma'am."

"Guess the acorn never falls far from the tree, does it?" she observes.

She walks up to Dad and grabs his cheeks. "You were such a great little singer. My music class was never the same after you left to play football. Your beautiful voice used to echo off the walls."

My Dad? A singer? No way. He's not so much as hummed in my direction in my whole life.

You would not believe it, but the old lady smiles so big her face looks like it's going to crack wide open.

She pulls hard on Dad's cheeks. "Will you sing for me, William?"

Dad stumbles back. "Oh, oh...I can't..."

"Why not?"

"I, I'm not a singer." Dad stutters.

Looking up to her, I say. "Trust me, he's not a singer."

She puts her hands on my shoulders. "Your father is the most wonderful singer I have ever heard. Bar none."

Then a sound comes from behind me, a wonderful sound.

I slowly turn around to see Dad moving his head side to side. Sounds I never heard before flow free from my old man's heart. The music is dancing in the air, engulfing the silence. This beautiful melody feels like it has been fighting to get out since long before I was born.

Dad's voice is going from high to low with ease. My old man doesn't even sing in the shower. I don't understand how he can sing like this. People on TV don't sing this good. The old lady's eyes roll back in her head like she just ate the best piece of chocolate she's ever had or she was a frog who had just munched down on a big old dragonfly. She waves her hands back and forth as Dad follows with his song. As Dad comes to the end, she slowly drops her arms and opens her eyes.

Dad says, "Ms. Hillbloom, like I said, in our family, everyone pulls his own. If Jack is up here after school playing piano, he is not making any money."

Ms. Hillbloom gazes out of the window as if she is pondering. Her eyes light up. "If you take 10 pounds of apples to the market, you can make $ 1.50 per pound."

"Really?" I say. I have no idea how much money that is, but it sounds like a lot.

Ms. Hillbloom says, "Really."

Dad nods his head. So do I. Then he says, "Thank you, ma'am."

He nudges my shoulders once, then twice. I screech.

"Oh yeah. Thank you, Ms. Hillbloom!"

On our way home, I try to add up in my mind how much money I'm going to make: 10 pounds...$1.50 per pound...

"Oh, I got it. 15 bucks!"

Dad glares over at me.

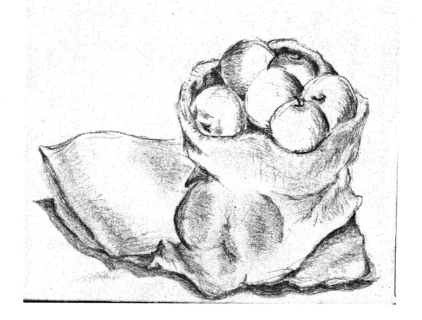

XI
DEALING WITH DANNY

He shows up early Monday morning on the porch. Maybe I'll duck out the back again. I can't play out the same old game anymore. I carry the diary everywhere I go now. I got me jobs all over town and people smile at me. My new task is to give all that money I took back. Yeah, I'm giving it back! It doesn't hurt so bad 'cause I have my own cash now. The Chinese storekeeper is letting me work off all the candy bars I took by cleaning the place twice a week.

"Danny, how are you?"

"OK." Danny looks at me like I have a fever or something. We sit there on the porch for what feels like an eternity.

Danny whispers. "Wanna make some money?"

I lean back. "I told you I can't do those things anymore."

Danny stands up. "Do what?"

I slide as far back in the chair as I can. "Take people's money."

Danny protests. "What's wrong with you? You've really changed since you got that dang book!"

I hug the backpack in my lap. "I know."

He grabs at it. "Gimmy that thing!"

I pull back. "No, Danny!" We tug back and forth.

Danny says, "Why not?"

"There's nothing we can do!"

Danny lets go of my pack. "Well, you can do whatever you want, but I'm going to get paid!"

The book rumbles in my backpack. Danny says, "I'm outta here."

I unzip the backpack as Danny walks away. Light spills out along with the voice of my diary: "Just because you stop, doesn't mean he will. You need to stay on your path."

I see Danny heading around the corner in the direction of Poindexter's house.

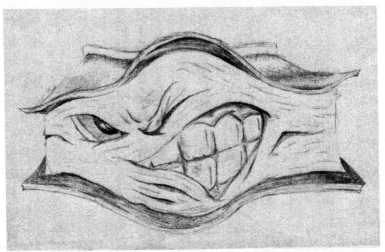

"The boy needs you," the diary says. I squint my eyes. "Why does he need me?"

The book's pages ruffle. "You taught Danny how to steal from people. He is your creation."

I thought to myself, "Damned if the book doesn't have a point. Danny would still be sitting on the sidelines really not bothering anybody if it hadn't been for me. My diary dims again, and its last muffled words are "Help him..."

So I run.

I get there just in time. Danny is just about to bear down on Poindexter with his fist. I feel like I've been through this a hundred times before. I stop the first swing with my hand.

Danny yells, "Get outta here, Jack!" He rips his hand free.

I step between them. Danny rears back and pops me. Well that's what I think he did. Awww, does this hurt!
I look up from the ground. Oh yeah, I forgot to tell you. I'm lying down now with Poindexter underneath me.

I say to Danny. "Leave Poindexter alone!" I'll bet Poindexter wishes now I'd just minded my own business. He pushes with all his might and yells, "Get off me, Jack!" He groans a little more. Danny bends over and pushes me back over as I try to get up.

He says, "You stay away from me or I'll belt you again!" I am in no position to protest. I watch Danny walk away.

Months have past and the diary hasn't said a word. It just sits there like a lump on a log. I don't even carry the thing with me anymore. I walk into my bedroom after the news of Mom and the new baby. She tells Dad and me at the same time. We look at each other thinking, "Is the diary going to show up for the baby too?"

Later that night, before I go to bed, my book began to sparkle and vibrate unlike ever before. The cover slowly opens. My book says, "You've done well, Jack. The time for us has passed. The person you are now is who you always will be."

Great, more riddles. I've just finally figured out the Indian guy's stuff.

My book says, "I have only one more thing for you, my friend."

"What is that?" My book had stopped telling me what to do months ago.

"Your path is set. I belong to another now. I will ask you because you now no longer need to be told."

"I'll do whatever you ask."

"I need to be placed in the hands of another."

I think to myself. Another? Who will this person be? Is this somebody I don't know? So many faces are going through my head. Beautiful colors sparkle over the pages of my book as it closes one page at a time. Each page becomes a spoken word. "Our brief time together created change not only in yourself but in people around you. Admire no one, because who you will become will hold admiration for all that come to know you." The last three pages fold over as the book says, "Be good Jack." Laughter rumbles over the closed pages.

The cover unwrites itself as if it's in reverse. The K slowly disappears one line at a time, the C follows, the A melds itself into oblivion, and the J creeps off the page as if it was never there. I say to the book. "I still don't know who to give it to." The book sits silently, but when I pick it up.

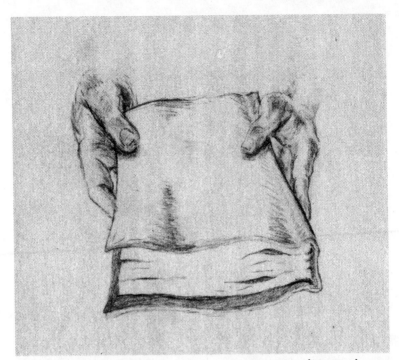

The book feels like someone is pushing down on its cover. Then a dark line appears from top to bottom, burning its face. A loop seals it, and a small circle begins in front of it. It's writing a name. D-a-n-n-y.

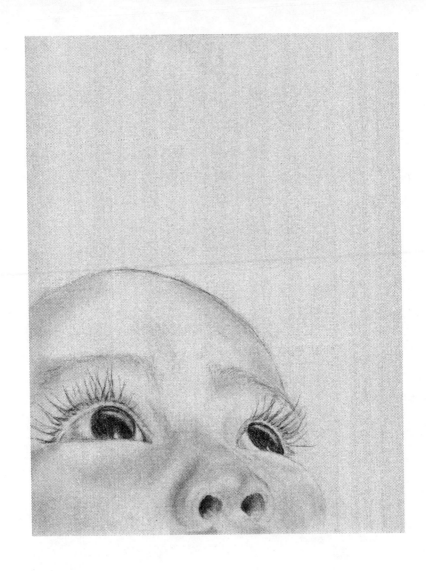

When the precipice of goodness looms far from your
heart ?

Special Thanks:

I would not be the person I am today without these people.
These folks were my Foster Parents that helped me out of a
rough spot. Folks I will always love and respect.
Thank you all.

Betsy & Gary McVean
Mack & Carolyn
Freddie Karcher
Jack Crawford
Eddy Cusac

This book was an eight year project that helped get me back to
my root drawing skills and my art foundation.

Thanks as well to my Editors and Special Facilitators:

Sarah Iselin
Mack Paul
Charles Odendhal IV
Ann Hall
and
Thom Renbarger
Cohort & Layout Designer

And all those who I can never name.

Please be sure and check out David Hall's first novel

"Broken From Within" 2012

Email brokenfromwithinpublications@gmail.com to purchase a
copy or go to Amazon.